MW00908542

THE CHRISTMAS BANDIT

by Lara Bergen
illustrated by Artful Doodlers

Ready-to-Read

Simon Spotlight

New York   London   Toronto   Sydney

Based on the TV series *Totally Spies!*™ created by
Marathon Animation as seen on Cartoon Network®. Series
created by Vincent Chalvon-Demersay and David Michel

SIMON SPOTLIGHT
An imprint of Simon & Schuster Children's Publishing Division
1230 Avenue of the Americas, New York, New York 10020

Library of Congress Cataloging-in-Publication Data
Bergen, Lara.
The Christmas Bandit / by Lara Bergen; illustrated by
Artful Doodlers.—1st ed.
p. cm.—(Ready-to-read. Level 2)
"Based on the TV series Totally Spies! created by
Marathon Animation as seen on Cartoon Network."
ISBN-13: 978-1-4169-0224-9 (pbk.)
ISBN-10: 1-4169-0224-4 (pbk.)
I. Artful Doodlers. II. Totally spies (Television program)
III. Title. IV. Series.
PZ7.B44985Chr 2005
(E)—dc22
2004028840

It was Christmas Eve morning.
Sam, Alex, and Clover had
a lot of shopping to do.
"I sure hope everyone else
is shopping this hard
for me!" said Clover.
"Oh, Clover!" said Sam.

"Look!" Alex said. "There is Santa!

Let's take our picture with him!"

"That is just a man in a suit,"

Clover said.

"Let's take our picture together
instead!" said Sam.

The girls climbed into
a nearby photo booth.
"Say 'cheese!'" Clover said.
Instead of snapping the picture,
the booth whisked them away!

They landed in front of
their spy boss, Jerry.

"Hello, spies," Jerry said.

"This had better be good!"
said Clover.

"We have so much Christmas
shopping to do!" Sam said.

"Sorry, girls," Jerry said, "but
there might not be a Christmas.
All over the world,
presents are disappearing
from under Christmas trees."
"No way!" said Clover.

"We have also picked up
odd activity at the south pole,"
Jerry said.
"Your mission is to go there
and see what is going on.

"Now for your gadgets . . .
X-ray Ski Goggles
with zoom lenses,
Laser Lipsticks,
and Bionic Boomerang
Bungee Mufflers.

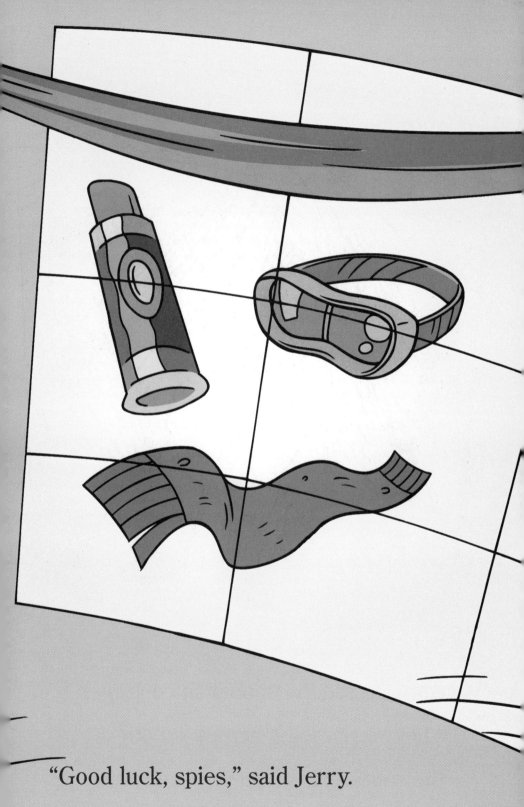

"Good luck, spies," said Jerry.

Hours later, the spies

were dressed in snowman costumes.

They were racing across

the south pole on jet-powered skis.

"Hey, what is that?" Alex said.

"It looks like some kind
of workshop," said Sam.

"What are you waiting for?"
Clover asked.

"Let's check it out!"

The spies took off their costumes
and hid behind a pile of snow.
Then they put on their
X-ray Ski Goggles with zoom lenses.

"Do you guys see what I see?"
Clover asked.

"Those little guys are
unwrapping presents!"

"Yeah—and that skinny guy
with the black beard is melting them
in that pot!" Sam said.

"We have to stop them!" Sam said.

The spies snuck up behind

the workshop.

Sam pulled out her Compowder.

"I am calling Jerry."

Then a skinny hand
grabbed Sam's Compowder.
The spies looked up.
It was the man
with the black beard!

Within minutes, the spies' feet
were trapped in blocks of ice.
"I will deal with you later,"
the villain told them.
"I have to destroy more gifts
before midnight!"

"But why do you want

to ruin Christmas?" Alex asked.

"Because Christmas was ruined

for me!" he said.

"When I was six years old
I asked Santa for a pony,"
the man told them.
"But all I got was an erector set!
I swore that one day I would
ruin Christmas for everyone!
And Santa's own elves helped me!"

"Santa's elves?" Alex asked.

"Yes, the elves Santa fired

for making bad toys," the man said.

"My plan is almost complete.

And you are not going to stop me!"

"You will never get away with this,"
Sam said.

"Just watch me!" he said
as he walked away.

"We cannot let him do this!"
Clover said.

"I have to get presents this year!"

"Let's use our Laser Lipsticks!"

Sam said.

The beams melted the ice,

and their feet were free.

"Time to give that villain a lesson
in Christmas spirit!" Sam said.
"Boomerang Mufflers—go!"
they shouted.

In a flash, the villain was caught.

"These Boomerang Mufflers

are way cool!" said Alex.

Now that the villain was caught,

it was time for a talk.

"Christmas is not just about

getting presents," Sam said.

"It's not?" Clover whispered.

"For sure! It's about love, family, and friends!" Alex said.

"And giving," Sam said.

"You should really try it."

"You are right. But I melted
all the gifts, and there's no time
to get new ones!" the villain said.
"Good point," said Alex as she
freed the villain.

"Hey! Do you hear what I hear?
It sounds like someone's
cell phone is ringing," Clover said.
"No, it sounds like . . .
sleigh bells!" said Sam.

They all ran outside.

"Hey, a note!" said Clover.

She handed it to the villain.

Dear Dagwood,

Do not worry about the gifts.

I have got it covered.

Christmas is all about sharing.

Work on giving to others,

and you might just find a pony

in your stocking next year.

Merry Christmas!

S.

Later the spies headed back home.

"Merry Christmas!" Dagwood called.

"Merry Christmas, Dagwood,"

the spies said.

And thanks to the spies

(and you-know-who)

it was the best Christmas ever!